Daniel Goes to the Carnival

Adapted by Angela C. Santomero
Based on the screenplay "The Neighborhood Carnival"
written by Dustin Ferrer
Poses and layouts by Jason Fruchter

Simon Spotlight
New York   London   Toronto   Sydney   New Delhi

SIMON SPOTLIGHT
An imprint of Simon & Schuster Children's Publishing Division
1230 Avenue of the Americas, New York, New York 10020
This Simon Spotlight paperback edition May 2017
© 2017 The Fred Rogers Company
All rights reserved, including the right of reproduction in whole or in part in any form.
SIMON SPOTLIGHT and colophon are registered trademarks of Simon & Schuster, Inc.
For information about special discounts for bulk purchases, please contact Simon & Schuster
Special Sales at 1-866-506-1949 or business@simonandschuster.com.
Manufactured in the United States of America 0617 LAK
10 9 8 7 6 5 4 3 2
ISBN 978-1-4814-7808-3
ISBN 978-1-4814-7809-0 (eBook)

Daniel hops on Trolley. "Will you take us to the Neighborhood Carnival, please?"

"*Ding! Ding!*" replies Trolley.

Daniel says, "I'm going to ride the great big Ferris wheel! Margaret is too little. But I'm big now. So I'm going to ride it for the first time!"

Daniel and Mom sing, "We're off to the carnival t
wheel. Won't you ride along with me? Ride along! W
along with me?"

"Wow!" says Daniel as they arrive at the carnival. He sees all sorts of games. Above it all, the Ferris wheel spins round and round. It looks like fun!

At the ducky game Daniel sees Miss Elaina.
"Hi, Miss Elaina!" Daniel says. "Will you ride the Ferris wheel with me?"
"Sure, Daniel!" she says. "It's going to be fun, fun, fun!"

Daniel and Miss Elaina run to the Ferris wheel. Daniel looks way up to the top of the ride. "Oh!" says Daniel. He didn't realize it was going to be so big.

Daniel stays behind as Miss Elaina hurries to get on the ride.
"What's wrong?" she asks. "Aren't you coming?"
"I'm not ready to go yet," Daniel says.
"Okay!" Miss Elaina says. "I'll go play a game instead."

Daniel looks down. Mom asks, "What's wrong, Daniel?"

"I don't know," he says. "I'm excited to ride the Ferris wheel. But I'm a little scared, too. I feel kind of . . . mixed-up."

Mom sings, *"Sometimes you feel two feelings at the same time, and that's okay."*

That makes Daniel feel better. He looks at the Ferris wheel. "Maybe I can ride the Ferris wheel later," he says.

"Step right up! Step right up! Come try our carnival ring toss game," says Prince Tuesday.

Daniel smiles. Playing a game will be grr-ific!

"A royal hello!" says Prince Wednesday. "Do you want to play this game with me? You have to toss the rings around the bottles."

"All right!" Daniel says.

"One, two, three, and *toss*!" they say. Tossing the rings is fun!

"That happens to me too sometimes," Daniel says. Then he sings, "Sometimes you feel two feelings at the same time, and that's okay."

"That makes me feel better," says Prince Wednesday, smiling. "Let's try again!"

Daniel and Prince Wednesday say, "One, two, three, and *toss*!" This time Prince Wednesday's ring makes it around a bottle. Hurray!

"Here's your prize," Prince Tuesday says.

"Bubbles!" exclaims Prince Wednesday.

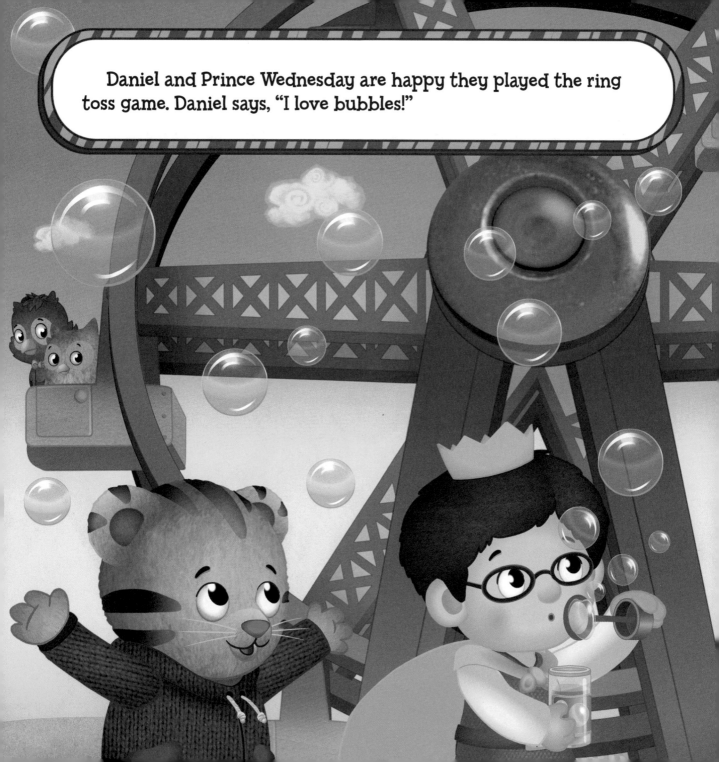

Daniel and Prince Wednesday are happy they played the ring toss game. Daniel says, "I love bubbles!"

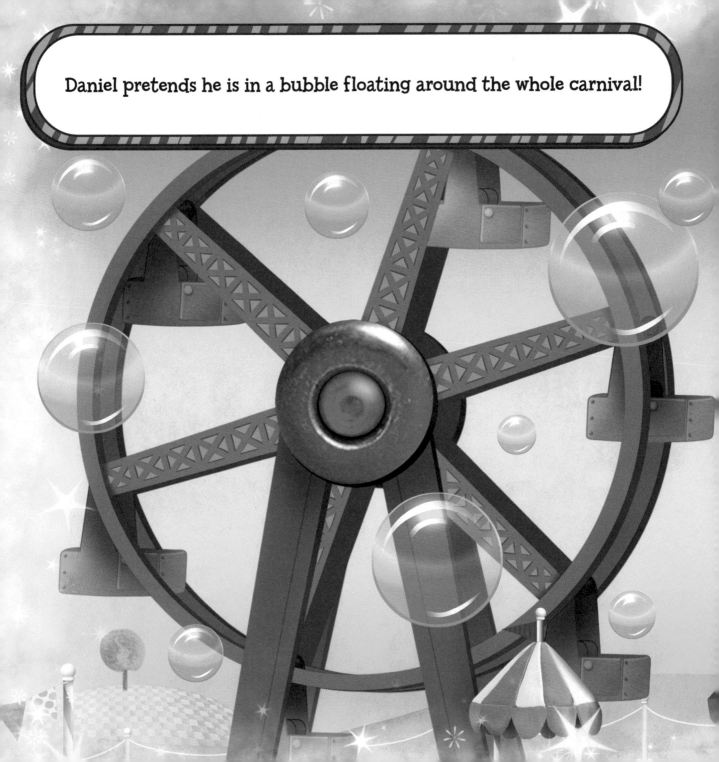

Daniel sings, "I'll float, float, float in my bubble, float up in the air, float here and float there! I can see the carnival as I float by! I love the view as I float in the sky!"

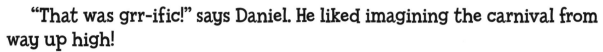

"That was grr-ific!" says Daniel. He liked imagining the carnival from way up high!

Miss Elaina runs over. "Hey, Daniel, are you ready to go on the Ferris wheel?" she asks.

"I think I'm ready to try!" Daniel says.

"Hurray!" Miss Elaina says.

"How do you feel about riding the Ferris wheel?" Mom asks Daniel. "I feel excited, and I feel a little scared," says Daniel. "But sometimes you feel two feelings at the same time, and that's okay. I'm ready to ride the Ferris wheel!"

Daniel, Miss Elaina, and Mom climb into the Ferris wheel car and buckle up. "Here we go!" Daniel says as the Ferris wheel starts to move. The car goes up, up, up! "Wheee, this is tiger-tastic!" cheers Daniel.